Monkey is Missing!

Contents

Written by Michaela Morgan

Illustrated by Elisa Rocchi

Collins

Who's in this story?

Listen and say

Grandma

James

Joy

Monkey

Download the audio at www.collins.co.uk/839746

Mum

Dad

🎧 2 Run for the train

One day, Joy, James, Mum, Dad and Grandma were at the train station. They wanted to go home.

"Quick!" shouted Dad. "The train is at 5 o'clock!"

"Oh no!" said Mum. "It's going."

"That was our train," said Grandma.

The children watched the train go.

"Don't worry," said Mum. "We can get a different train."

"When is that?" asked Joy.

"I can ask," said Mum.

"What time is the train, please?" Mum asked.

"The train is at six o'clock from **platform** 9," said the man at the **information desk**.

"OK. We can wait," said Mum.

"Grandma, Joy and James can wait with all the bags in the **waiting room**," said Mum. "Dad and I can buy some **snacks** and something to drink."

The waiting room

In the waiting room, there were lots of people. There were tall people, small people, old people and young people.

The people weren't very happy and they weren't very **friendly**. They didn't say hello. It was very quiet.

"Don't make too much noise," Grandma said to the children.

Grandma put her bags on a table. It was very hot in the waiting room. She took off her big coat, her scarf and her big hat.

Joy and James took some things from their bags and started to play with them.

They had drawing books, pens and pencils,
puzzle books, books to read and Monkey.

Monkey was Joy's favourite toy.

A small boy wanted to play with Monkey, but Joy loved her toy very much. Grandma gave Monkey to her when she was a small baby.

Now the small boy wanted the drawing book.
But he wanted to eat the book!

James took the drawing book from him.

"Sorry, you can't eat that!" he said.

Where is monkey?

All the people in the waiting room waited and waited.

A boy in the waiting room said, "Ten past five, twenty past five, twenty-five past five, half past five ..."

"*Shh!*" said his mother.

Dad and Mum came with the snacks. James and Joy stopped playing with their things and started eating. They had sandwiches, orange juice, chocolate cake and an apple.

Mum had the tickets.

Dad watched the bags. But …

"Oh no!" said Joy. "I can't find Monkey. Where is he?"

"Is he on the seat?" asked Mum.

"No!" said Joy.

"Is he under the seat?" said Grandma.

"No!" said Joy. "Where is he?"

"Is he in the **rubbish bin**?" said Joy.

"No!" said James. "That's very dirty!"

"WASH YOUR HANDS!" said Grandma. "Now!"

Joy was very sad, but she went to wash her hands.

After Joy washed her hands, she thought she saw Monkey.

"Here he is!" she shouted, but ...

... it was a girl's hair!

"Oh, sorry! Excuse me!" said Joy.

"Is that monkey?" Joy asked.

But, no, it was part of a coat.

"Excuse me! I'm sorry," Joy said.

"There's Monkey!" said Joy. "I found you ... ."

"*Woof!*" said a dog.

"Oh!" cried Joy. "You aren't Monkey."

Dad looked at the **departures board**.

"Quick, let's go!" he said. "Quick, let's go!"

But Joy didn't want to get on the train.

"Where's Monkey? I want to find Monkey!"
she said.

Help!

Then James had an idea.

"Please can you all help?" James asked the people in the waiting room. "We need to find a toy monkey."

All the people stood up and started to look for Monkey.

Is Monkey ...
... up there?
... in there?
... behind there?
... on top of there?

22

The people in the waiting room were friendly now, but they couldn't find Monkey.

Joy was very, very sad.

"We're sorry. We can buy a new monkey," said Mum.

"I don't want a new monkey," said Joy. "I want my old Monkey."

"Let's go home, Joy," said Grandma.

"Let's be quick!" said Dad.

Grandma put on her coat, her scarf and her hat.

"Oh!" she said. "Who's sleeping in my hat?"

"Look! That small boy made a bed for Monkey!" said Joy. James laughed.

Run for the train ... again!

"Let's go!" said Mum. "Quick. Run!"

Gran put on her hat, Dad picked up the bags, James took the books and Mum got the tickets.

Joy was careful. She didn't drop Monkey!

And they ran and ran!

"There's platform seven," said Joy.

"There's platform eight," said James.

"And here's platform nine!" said Mum.

They walked onto platform nine,
and Dad said ...

"The train is going!"

"Oh no!" said James.

"That was our train," said Joy.

"OK. We can wait," said Mum.

"Let's go to the waiting room again,"
said Grandma.

Now all the people were very friendly.

"Hello again!" they said.

"Would you like to sit down?" a man said to Grandma.

"We didn't get the train," said Joy, "but we found Monkey!"

"And we've made lots of friends," said James.

Mini-dictionary

Listen and read

departures board (noun)
The **departures board** is the sign in a train station that shows where trains are going and when they leave.

friendly (adjective)
Someone who is **friendly** behaves in a pleasant and kind way.

information desk (noun)
An **information desk** is a place in a train station where you can go to find things out.

platform (noun)
The **platform** is the area in a train station where you get on and off a train.

puzzle (noun) A **puzzle** is a fun question that is difficult to answer. You can buy a book that has lots of puzzles in it.

rubbish bin (noun)
A **rubbish bin** is a container that you put things you don't want in.

snack (noun) A **snack** is a small, simple meal that is quick to make and to eat.

waiting room (noun) A **waiting room** is a room in a train station where people can sit down while they wait.

1 Look and order the story.

2 Listen and say

Collins

Published by Collins
An imprint of HarperCollins*Publishers*
Westerhill Road
Bishopbriggs
Glasgow
G64 2QT

HarperCollins*Publishers*
1st Floor, Watermarque Building
Ringsend Road
Dublin 4
Ireland

William Collins' dream of knowledge for all began with the publication of his first book in 1819.

A self-educated mill worker, he not only enriched millions of lives, but also founded a flourishing publishing house. Today, staying true to this spirit, Collins books are packed with inspiration, innovation and practical expertise. They place you at the centre of a world of possibility and give you exactly what you need to explore it.

© HarperCollins*Publishers* Limited 2020

10 9 8 7 6 5 4 3 2

ISBN 978-0-00-839746-3

Collins® and COBUILD® are registered trademarks of HarperCollins*Publishers* Limited

www.collins.co.uk/elt

British Library Cataloguing in Publication Data

A catalogue record for this publication is available from the British Library.

Author: Michaela Morgan
Illustrator: Elisa Rocchi (Beehive)
Series editor: Rebecca Adlard
Commissioning editors: Fiona Undrill and Zoë Clarke
Publishing manager: Lisa Todd
Product managers: Jennifer Hall and Caroline Green
In-house editor: Alma Puts Keren
Project manager: Emily Hooton
Editor: Matthew Hancock
Proofreaders: Natalie Murray and Michael Lamb
Cover designer: Kevin Robbins
Typesetter: 2Hoots Publishing Services Ltd
Audio produced by id audio, London
Reading guide author: Emma Wilkinson
Production controller: Rachel Weaver
Printed and bound by: GPS Group, Slovenia

Download the audio for this book and a reading guide for parents and teachers at www.collins.co.uk/839746